Talking About Time

How Long Does It Take?

Jilly Attwood

Raintree

Chicago, Illinois

© 2005 Raintree
Published by Raintree, a division of Reed Elsevier, Inc.
Chicago, Illinois
Customer Service 888-363-4266
Visit our website at www.raintreelibrary.com

Printed and bound by South China Printing Company.
09 08 07 06 05
10 9 8 7 6 5 4 3 2 1

Library of Congress Cataloging-in-Publication Data:

Attwood, Jilly.
  Talking about time : how long does it take? / Jilly Attwood.
    p. cm.
  ISBN 1-4109-1639-1 (library binding-hardcover) -- ISBN 1-4109-1645-6 (pbk.)
  1. Time perception--Juvenile literature. I. Title.
  BF468.A77 2005
  153.7'53--dc22

                              2004025607

Acknowledgments
The publishers would like to thank the following for permission to reproduce photographs: Alamy p. **18**; Corbis pp. **13**, **23b** (Lester Lefkowitz), **19** (Ariel Skelley), **12**, **23a** (Jennie Woodcock/ Refections Photolibrary); Digital Vision p. **7** (Rob Van Petten); Harcourt Education pp. **10-11**, **20**, **21** (Gareth Boden), **15** (Trevor Clifford), **8** (Chris Honeywell); Tudor Photography pp. **9**, **16**, **17**, **14**.

Cover photograph reproduced with permission of Corbis (Tom and Dee Ann McCarthy).

Every effort has been made to contact copyright holders of any material reproduced in this book. Any omissions will be rectified in subsequent printings if notice is given to the publishers.

Some words are shown in bold, **like this**. You can find out what they mean by looking in the glossary on page 24.

Contents

Getting Ready for School

Niran zips his jacket.

Zip!

4

He buttons his coat.
Which takes more **time**?

Going to School

David and his mom walk to school.

Sarah and her dad ride bikes to school.

Who will take **longer**? David and his mom take longer.

7

George has a
big bucket.

Jenny has a
small bucket.

Which bucket will fill
more quickly?

George filled his bucket quickly.
But Jenny was **quicker**.

Play Time

Does it take longer to climb up or to slide down?

Wheeee!

Sports Day

Who will win the race?

Which is quicker,
a running race or a sack race?

At Home

What is quicker?

Taking your shoes off...

Rip!

...or putting them on?

Baking

These children are making bread.
Have you made bread?

stir!

The bread is baked.

Yum, yum!

Making bread takes longer than eating bread!

17

Dog Time

Peter brushes
his dog.

David washes his dog.

Which takes longer?
Brushing or washing?

Bed Time

Sheryl brushes her teeth and washes her face.

Which takes longer?

How Long Does It Take?

Which is longer?
Which is faster?

OR

OR

OR

23

Glossary

longer   talking more time
quicker   taking less time
time   how long something takes

Index

bread 16, 17

brush 18, 20, 21

coat 5

dog 17, 18

race 12, 13

sand 8, 9

shoes 14, 15

slide 10, 11

walk 6

Notes for adults

The *Talking about time* series introduces young children to the concept of time. By relating their own experiences to specific moments in time, the children can start to explore the pattern of regular events that occur in a day, week or year.

This book explores the passing of time of activities familiar to children. For each set of activities it asks the reader to consider which of the two takes the longer or shorter time to do. The book provides an opportunity for children, in a classroom or home situation, to try out the activities for themselves to consolidate their understanding of concepts associated with time such as longer, shorter, quicker.

Follow-up activities

Use a stop-watch to measure how long it takes a child to do various linked activities, e.g. zipping up a jacket and buttoning up a jacket; climbing up a slide and sliding down it.
Before filling up different-sized containers, such as buckets, with sand, ask your child to predict which ones will take the longest and shortest time to fill up and why.